What Should We Do Today?

Written by Lisa Rao
Illustrated by Susan Hall
Book Design by Michael Dawson

Based on the TV series DORA THE EXPLORER as seen on Nick Jr.

Nick Jr./Dynatech
© 2006 Viacom International Inc. All rights Reserved.
Manufactured in TK
2 4 6 8 10 9 7 5 3 1
ISBN TK

Today is a perfect day for exploring! The sun is shining, and there isn't a cloud in the sky.

Dora can't wait to see her best friend, Boots, and set out on a new adventure!

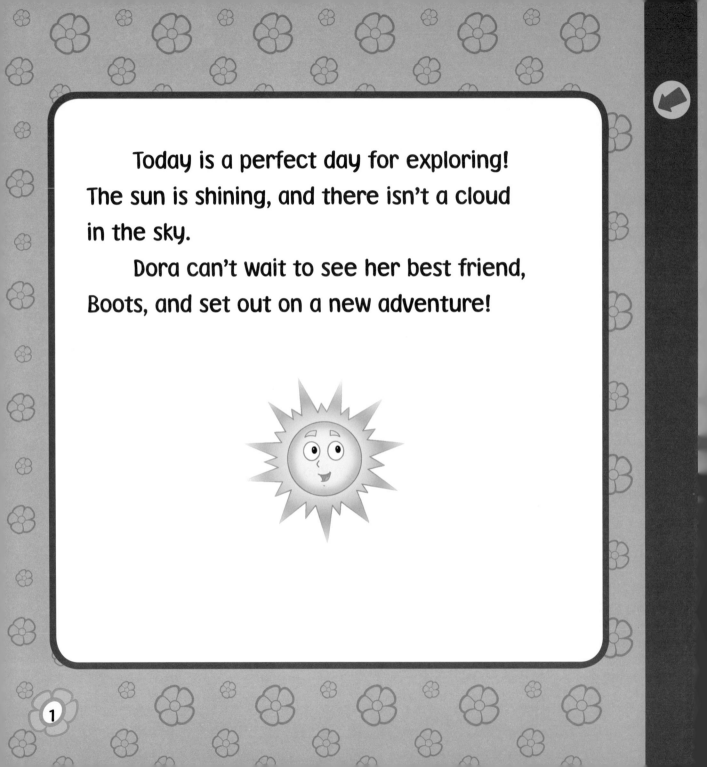

Dora runs outside, where Boots is waiting for her.

"*¡Hola*, Boots! Ready for an adventure today?" Dora asks.

"Yeah, yeah, yeah!" Boots cheers. "But, Dora! How do we decide what to do on our adventure today?"

Dora has an idea. She goes inside and comes back out carrying a big, fat book. "I brought my photo album," she explains. "Maybe looking at the pictures in it will help us decide what to do today."

Dora opens the album. Boots points at the first page.

"Dora! These are pictures of us at the beach!" he exclaims. "I love the beach! I love building sandcastles and collecting shells and digging in the sand!"

"Me too, Boots," says Dora. "It's great to play at the beach, get really hot, and then jump in the cold water!"

"Yeah! Going to the beach is the best!" Boots cheers. "Let's go on a beach adventure!"

But, before Dora can answer, a breeze flips the page of Dora's photo album.

"Ooooh! There's a picture of us riding in Tico's car!" Boots says. "I love riding in Tico's car!"

"Me too, Boots," says Dora. "I love going on a car adventure, and waving to our friends as we drive past."

"Going for a ride with Tico is great!" Boots crows. "Let's go on a car adventure with Tico!"

Dora flips to the next page in the photo album.

"Here was another great day," she says. "Remember when we went on a picnic at Play Park?"

"Your Abuela made us the best peanut butter and banana sandwiches," Boots remembers. "Yum!"

"¡Delicioso!" Dora agrees. "I love picnics! I even love it when our ant friends stop by for a snack!"

"Maybe we should go on a picnic adventure today, Dora!" Boots suggests.

Boots flips to the next photo in the album.

"Dora, look!" Boots says, pointing. "We're canoeing!"

"Yeah, remember the crocodiles? We had to paddle around them to get across Crocodile Lake," Dora says.

"That was exciting," says Boots. "Let's go on a canoe adventure today, Dora!"

Dora turns the page. "Look! Here's a picture of us at the Animal Rescue Center with my cousin, Diego," she says.

"Diego's so cool," Boots says. "He's a great Animal Rescuer."

"And he knows everything about animals!" Dora says.

"We can go see Diego and Baby Jaguar at the Animal Rescue Center," says Boots. "And maybe we'll even help them rescue an animal in trouble!"

Boots recognizes the next photo right away. "Hey, here we are in the Flowery Garden," he says.

"Yeah, the Flowery Garden is full of places to explore," says Dora.

"Maybe Isa will help us find some flowers to bring home to our mommies!" says Boots. "Let's go explore in Isa's Flowery Garden!"

Dora points to another photo.

"Ooooh, remember this?" Dora asks. "This was our big soccer game!"

"Yeah, I remember that game," Boots says. "Our team played really well! And you scored the winning goal, Dora!"

"I couldn't have done it without that great pass from you, Boots!" Dora reminds him.

"Maybe we should play soccer with our friends today," says Boots.

Dora turns to the next photo in the book.

"Remember this?" she asks Boots.

"Sure I do," Boots says. "We had a big party with all of our friends."

"And when we broke open the piñata, lots of treats spilled out," Dora says.

"Oooh, those treats were good!" Boots says. "Let's have a party today, Dora! What could be better than a party?" Boots is so excited he starts to dance!

Dora grins, then starts to turn the page. But there are no more pages to turn!

"Hey! That's the end of the pictures, Boots," Dora says. "I guess it's time to decide what to do today."

"So what should we do, Dora?" Boots asks again.

"Let's make a list," Dora suggests. "We could go to the beach, go for a drive, have a picnic, go on a canoe adventure, visit Diego, explore the Flowery Garden, play soccer or have a party!"

"Wow, Dora, that's a lot," Boots says.

Dora nods. "I'd like to do any of those things, but I don't think we can do all of them in one day," she says.

"Well, we need to do something, Dora," Boots says. "We always go on great adventures together!"

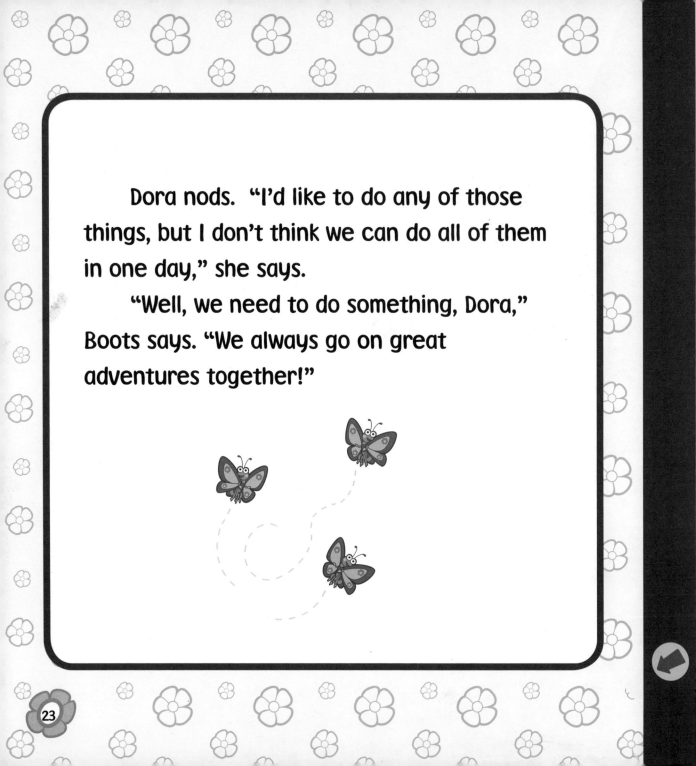

"Maybe all our adventures are so great because we go on them together!" Dora answers.

"Yeah, yeah, yeah! That's it, Dora," Boots cheers.

"So what should we do today, Boots?" Dora asks.

"We can do anything as long as we do it together!" Boots replies. "It will be a great day because I'm going to be with you!"